The Art of Forgiveness

Tanisha Hall

Simply Candice Marie LLC

ISBN: 9781728749617

DEDICATION

This book is dedicated to all the people I had to forgive and all the people who had to forgive me.

Forgiveness is something you must do if you want the joy-filled life God has for you.

The Art of **Forgive**ness

IN LOVING MEMORY

My Mother Sandra Hall, My Aunt Karen Larks, and My Uncle Michael Hall

This book is in memory of the best mother Sandra Hall. My mother had a heart of gold and would do anything for anyone. She was an awesome mother, magnificent grandmother, excellent sister, devoted cousin, wonderful friend, and great neighbor. She left us on September 15, 2019, and we miss her so much. We were not ready to say goodbye, but we are so grateful she is resting in peace. We love you Queen.

In memory of my Aunt Karen Larks. She was one of the sweetest people I knew. She was always there when you needed her. Every time I called her, she gave me a listening ear and the best sound advice. I miss her smile and her laugh. I also miss seeing her pass by and blowing while we were sitting on the porch. It's always in my mind when you rode with her, she would be singing her gospel songs. I love you forever. You will always be my funky butt.

Also, in memory of my Uncle Michael Hall. He had the kindest spirit. I did not get to see him much but whenever he could come down, we always had a good laugh. I will miss his quietness and the way he would say my mom's name. He did not talk much but he had an exceptionally beautiful smile. I love you Uncle Michael and you will always be in my heart and mind.

ACKNOWLEDGMENTS

To My Heavenly Father, thank you for loving me and sending your Son to die for me and letting your Holy Spirit dwell in me. Thank You for giving my spark back to write. I love you and will always speak of your awesome wonders.

To my son Skyler, I love you so much and I thank God for blessing my life with you. Thank you for giving momma some "me" time. You are going to be an amazing engineer and do great things for God's Kingdom. I love you more than words can say. You will always be my doodle.

To my brothers Brandon and TJ, thank you guys for being amazing. I love you and I will always have your back. You all are wonderful uncles and one-of-a-kind brothers. Thanks for always being there for me and Skyler.

A NOTE FROM THE AUTHOR

I wrote this book because there are so many people who are filled with guilt, bitterness, hatred, and pain. The Bible tells us if we want God to forgive us our trespasses, we must first forgive those who have trespassed against us.

I know it hurts and seems as if it is not getting better. I promise once you forgive others and yourself, your life will change for the better.

The enemy wants you to hold on to the hurt people have caused you and the things you have done in your past. He knows that once you see yourself as God sees you there will be nothing to stop you from getting to your destiny.

I finally forgave myself for something I did 11 years ago. I used to cry every night because I thought God would never love me again. I forgave myself because I realized that God had forgiven me the moment I repented, and it was time for me to forgive myself.

If you have unforgiveness in your heart, I pray you release it to God and let Him heal you and give you joy and peace.

Keep God first, keep your head up, and never forget that I love you. Thank you for your support.

Much Love,

Tanisha "Nisha" Hall

PART 1 | BROKEN AND BITTER

Summer

It has been two months and I haven't heard from Caleb. You'll think he would answer my calls or send me a card or put money on my books.

The more I sit in this cell, the more I think about the pain I'm going to cause him.

Caleb and I met 5 years ago at his cousin's wedding. I know I wanted to be with him the moment I laid eyes on him.

He was part of the wedding party, and he was wearing that suit just right. We ended up next to each other in the line to get a glass of wine.

"Hi there, beautiful. My name is Caleb."

"Hi Caleb, I'm Summer. It's very nice to meet you."

"Nice to meet you also. Are you here for Candace or Justin?"

"I'm here with Kelsey who's here for Candace."

"Well Ms. Summer, maybe you can save me a dance."

"I think that can be arranged, Mr. Caleb."

We ate, danced, and talked the night away. He asked me for my number and said he would call but I didn't hold my breath on it.

However, he did call a couple of days later, and I was surprised.

"Good morning Summer this is Caleb."

"Good morning I'm surprised that you called."

"Sorry I didn't get a chance to call yesterday. My aunt is in the hospital, and I went up there to check on her. My dad was tired, so I let him go home to get some rest and I stayed there."

"I'm so sorry to hear that. How is she doing?"

"Aunt Alice is very strong. She had the flu but she's better now."

"I'm glad to hear that. Thank God she's doing better."

"Thank God indeed. I was hoping to make it up to you later if you're not busy."

"Sure, what do you have in mind?"

"Can you meet me at the restaurant by the mall around 5?"

"Yes, I can meet you there."

"Thanks for being so understanding Summer."

"It's not a problem. I'll see you later.

We had a good time and Caleb was a real gentleman.

I thought he would never let any harm come to me. That is until we were pulled over by the police one day.

Caleb picked me up so we could go to the mall. He said we had to stop by one of his friend's houses.

We left his friend and headed to the mall. We were about 5 minutes away when we heard sirens and saw flashing lights.

He started looking out the rearview mirror and seemed nervous.

"Baby I need you to be down for me."

"I've been down for you since day one Caleb."

"I need you to say that these pills are yours. It's your first offence so you'll only get probation for about 2 years."

I loved Caleb so much and trusted everything he said. I just knew that if I did this for him, he would have my back.

"I'll do it only if you're sure I'm only going to get probation."

"Baby I promise I will never mislead you or lie to you."

That should have been my red flag. I took the bag of pills and put it in my pocket. The police came and asked Caleb for his license and registration. He said he pulled us over because we yield at the stop sign instead of coming to a complete stop.

When he came back from running Caleb's name and plate, he saw some small bags on the floor and told us to get out of the car.

He asked if he could search the car and Caleb gave him permission. After not finding anything, he searched Caleb and called for a female cop to come search me.

The cop came and found the pills. She handcuffed me and put me in the back of her car.

Caleb told me not to worry and he was coming down to bail me out. Well, I didn't get a bail and I didn't get probation. I received a sentence of two years.

Like I said, it's been two months since I've heard from him. I just sit in my cell plotting my revenge. I just want to do my time and find Caleb so I can hurt him the way he hurt me.

Jurnee

I'm sitting here at my cousin's party smiling but deep down I'm hurting.

I know my family doesn't like me and when I'm not around they talk about me.

Today we're at my aunt's house for my cousin Autumn's birthday party. I was asked to bring some ice and drinks. When they saw I had Sprite and Dr. Pepper they looked at me and rolled their eyes. Guess they wanted some alcohol or something.

Autumn hugged and thanked me for what I had brought. The rest of the family went inside, and I was left outside alone.

"Autumn comes inside so we can sing Happy Birthday to you," my Aunt Elizabeth said.

"Ok Jurnee and I will be right there," Autumn replied.

My aunt rolled her eyes and slammed the door. I picked up my plate and cup and threw them away.

"Autumn I love you and hope you enjoy the rest of your day. I have to get going but thanks again for inviting me."

"Jurnee, please don't go yet. I still have to open up my gifts."

I gave her the gift I had and told her I would text her when I made it home.

When I got into my car, I tried hard to hold back the tears. Soon as I made it to the interstate tears were streaming down my face.

I got home and texted Autumn then took a bubble bath. As I was laying in the tub relaxing, I started wondering why it is that my family hates me so much.

Guess it doesn't matter that I've helped them pay their bills, babysit their kids, clean their homes, and so much more.

"God please take this pain and hurt away from me. I just don't understand what I've done to deserve this."

I finished my bath and got into my favorite PJs. Got my wine and a piece of cake and put my favorite movie into the DVD player.

I fell asleep on the sofa and when I woke up, I had missed calls and a message from my Aunt Elizabeth.

"Jurnee next Friday is my Anniversary party. I was calling to see if you could bring some ice, drinks, meatballs, sandwiches, deviled eggs, chips and dip, and go half with me on the cake. Call me when you get this message."

Really? I was just at your house, and you were acting like you didn't want me there.

No matter if I help or not, they will still talk about me. I'm just going to get a couple of things and drop it off.

My phone started to ring but I let it go to voicemail. I was crying too much, and they would not understand what I was saying.

Someone had left a voicemail and when I checked it was my Aunt Elizabeth and cousin talking about me. They must have pocket dialed me.

"Girl you know Jurnee just got a promotion at work. If I were you, I would've asked her to buy everything I needed for my party."

"If she gets everything, I'll just have to get decorations."

"She has the money so she can't say she won't be able to do it."

I'm not good enough to sit at your house but my money is good enough to spend on you.

Just can't seem to put my finger on exactly what it is about me that they hate so much. At the age of 10 I noticed that I was treated differently. I always felt like I wasn't in the right family.

Every time they hear something about me, they just have to repeat it. I try hard to fit in, I just can't seem to.

I remember when I was younger, I worked so hard on a Christmas gift for my cousin. She put it in the trash when she thought I wasn't looking.

Maybe I've tried too hard to get them to like me. Since they want to repeat what they've heard about me, maybe I should find a way to tell them things that I know about them. Some things they have no clue I know.

I know exactly who to start with.

Aniya

This is the third time I've woken up from a nightmare drenched in sweat. I thought a mother was supposed to protect her children. Not my mother, she's anything but a protector.

Since the age of 11 she has pimped me out. To whom you might ask? Her friends, her dealers, even our family members.

I remember asking her why I had to show her I loved her in that way. After that she didn't feed me for two weeks.

She never hit me because she didn't want to draw attention to the situation.

The first time she pimped me I had just come home from school. She walked out of her bedroom with a strange look on her face.

"Aniya do you love your momma?"

"Yes, momma you know I love you."

"Momma needs you to show her your love."

"What do you mean show you?"

"Our lights are about to be cut off. My friend said he'll give us the money if you let him touch your legs."

"Momma! Why would you tell a man he can touch on your daughter?"

"Don't act like you're a virgin I came home early last week and heard you and that Darville boy in your room having sex."

"Momma we can't get the money any other way?"

"No baby, we need the money right now."

I put my head down and walked in her room. Her friend was on the bed without clothes on.

He told me to shut the door and to come sit down by him. When he finished what he was doing I ran out of that room so fast.

I got in the shower and scrubbed so hard that I started to bleed. I held myself and started crying. Later my mom came into my room and told me it was ok, and I started to feel a little better.

It didn't register at that moment that I had just been pimped out by my own mother.

A few months later she said I had to show my love again because the rent was due. This time a different man was in her room.

I wondered if other girls showed their mom's love in this way. The pain was beginning to be unbearable, so I started cutting myself.

My friends noticed a change in me and became concerned.

One weekend I slept by my best friend Amiya's house. I trusted her and told her what was going on.

"I can ask my mom if you can stay with us."

"Thanks Amiya but my mom would cause problems for us."

"Aniya you can't stay there!"

"I know and I'm trying to find a way out."

"You know I have your back."

"I know you do, and I thank you for that. Please don't tell anyone."

"I promise to never tell a soul."

On Monday morning Amiya told Mrs. Hill our Guidance Counselor. When I got to fifth period Child Protective Services was waiting for me in the office.

They asked me all types of questions but all I could do was cry. I was brought to the hospital and my mom was called to meet us there.

My mom told me everything was going to be all right and she was going to do what she had to so I could come back to her.

I was put in foster care and my mom, and I had scheduled weekly visits. Sometimes she came but didn't spend the full two hours with me.

As time passed on, she stopped coming. I would write her letters, but they always came back unopened.

One night I was in my room doing homework and I started wondering why my mom didn't love me anymore. I got a bottle of pills and took them. I told Amiya when I got to school the next day.

Once again, she promised not to tell anyone, but she told our Principal Mr. Wes. He called my social worker Ms. Katelyn, and she came and got me from school and brought me to the E.R.

The doctor pumped my stomach and said I was going to be fine, but my kidneys would have been messed up if I didn't get there when I did.

I told Ms. Katelyn I wanted to move out of the same city as my mom.

Now I'm 32 years old sitting here with a letter from my mom. All these years and now she wants to write to me?

She must want something, but I don't care what it is. All the pain she has caused me and now she wants to communicate?

Whatever!!

Summer

I had just finished getting my hair braided when the guard told me I had a visitor. I wondered who it could be since no one comes to see me.

I wish it would be Caleb but that would be too good to be true. My best friend Kelsey lives out of state, so I know it's not her.

It better not be one of Caleb's goons coming to do his dirty work. Maybe it's my new lawyer. I had to fire the other one. He was never prepared for court and I hardly saw him.

When I turned the corner, I didn't see anyone. Then I heard someone say, "Hey Mimi over here."

Mimi was the name Caleb gave me when we first started dating. When I turned the corner, I saw Isaac smiling at me. Isaac is one of Caleb's good friends. I never understood how they became so close because they are night and day.

"Hey Mimi, how are you holding up?"

"I'm good and I see your boy sent you to do his job."

"Caleb didn't send me, I came to check up on you because I wanted to."

"Stop playing Isaac. I know he sent you so he wouldn't have to face me."

"For real Summer I came to make sure you're straight. I also put some money in your account because I know how you like to eat and snack late at night."

"Thanks, I appreciate it more than you know. Where is Caleb? I haven't heard from him in 2 months?"

"Honestly, I haven't spoken to him in a minute. Your boy has been acting real crazy lately."

"Oh, my goodness what has he done now?"

"He's moving on other people's turf and being really careless. I told him to chill, and he went left on me."

"You know how Caleb is."

"Well, I'm good without him. He told his whole crew he didn't need us anymore. I said cool and bounced."

"That's too crazy. He better chill out before his tail is locked up for a long time."

"Yep, and you're right. I asked him when he was coming to see you and he told me to mind my business. I knew he would never come up here. That is why I came to check on you myself. I'm done with him and the street game."

"Now you tell that to someone who doesn't know you, Isaac Washington."

"I'm serious baby girl. I called my uncle who's out of state and he's going to get me an interview at the plant where he works."

"You're talking about your Uncle Kamryn?"

"The one and only. Besides, I'm getting too old for the streets. Time to grow up and handle my business."

"Well, I'm happy for you and wish you nothing but the best."

"Thanks, that means a lot to me coming from you. How have you been?"

"I'm good, I stay to myself, and I started taking classes to get my time reduced."

"For what it's worth, you're more of a man than Caleb will ever be. If you were my girl, I would have taken my own charge."

"You're just trying to make me feel better."

"I'm so serious right now. If you need anything my number is still the same. I'm going home and getting some things together to go out to my uncles. I'm going to check on you when I get back."

"Thanks again for coming up here."

"Keep your head up and remember that I will always have your back."

As I walked back to my cell I started thinking. How is it my man hasn't made his way up here to see me, but his friend has? That just let me know what type of person he really is.

He's not a real man because just like Isaac said I should not be here. I'm so proud of Isaac for getting his life back on track.

When I do see Caleb, it will not be anything nice.

Jurnee

When I woke up this morning, I had a text message from my Aunt Elizabeth. No, she didn't have the nerves to ask me to buy more stuff for her party.

This family is really getting on my last nerve. I am crying because I know they hate me, yet my money is good enough for them.

I start plotting in my head how I'm going to spill all the tea on them. Now they will have something to talk about.

I open my notebook and start writing everything I know about all of them. Maybe I should make flyers and hang all around town. I wonder how much a build board will be.

I've put up with their hatred long enough. While I'm crying at night wondering what I did to them, they are in bed sound asleep.

A few months ago, I brought some crawfish and decided to go by my cousin's house. When her daughter opened the door and said my name everyone sighed so loudly. When they saw the crawfish, their attitudes changed.

I didn't stay, I just gave them the food and left. On another occasion my aunt had gone to the doctor, and I called to check on her. She acted as if it was going to kill her to talk to me.

Two days later she called me to see if I could babysit for her. Until this day I have yet to get paid. Sometimes I daydream that I'm not really part of this family.

Last night I dreamed that my entire family came to my house. They had cake and gifts and food, and I asked them what was going on.

They said they came by to thank me for all that I do for them. One of my oldest cousins got up and made a toast.

"Jurnee, we love you and are so glad that you're a part of our family. You do so much for us, and you go above and beyond to help everyone. We just wanted to let you know that we appreciate you and all that you do. You're truly one of a kind."

I woke up with a smile on my face. Maybe one day they will like me. I really don't understand what it is about me that they don't like.

I live in a mobile home while they are sitting pretty in beautiful 2 and 3 story homes. They got their cars from dealerships, and I bought mine from someone's yard. I'm single with no kids and they're married with beautiful children.

The only one who truly is there for me is my cousin Autumn. I've cried to her about this family so much that now I get bad headaches.

I'm going to come up with the best way to expose them all. Maybe then their attitude towards me will change.

Aniya

After I got up and got dressed, I headed to my hair appointment. Everyone I saw told me they were sorry to hear about my mom.

What were they talking about?

I just said thank you and kept walking. When I walked in the beauty shop Amiya was there in one of the seats getting her hair done.

I haven't spoken to her since high school when she told our secret and lost my trust.

I say good morning, sign in and wait to be seen. Amiya keeps looking my way but doesn't say anything. She was my only friend and I trusted her with my life.

I never thought for a moment that she would betray me the way she did. As I pass her to go to my seat, she says hi to me in a low voice. I act as if I didn't hear her and keep walking.

My stylist Janet tells me she's sorry to hear about my mom. I'm curious to know what everyone keeps being sorry about. I tell her thanks and start talking about the shooting that happened up the street.

"Janet, you heard what happened the other day at the basketball court?"

"Girl that was those young boys from 8th street."

"I heard it was over a girl. These young kids today are too much."

"Aniya keep still before this straightener get you neck. Now that's too sad to shoot somebody over a girl."

"Nikki said he's doing good and should be coming home soon."

"That's good and I pray our young people get it together soon rather than later."

"Hopefully, this will make them go to school like they are supposed to."

We talked and laughed about what it was like when we were growing up. I paid Janet, looked at Amiya and walked out.

I wanted to tell her I was still hurt because of what she did, but I decided not to waste my time.

Nothing was on TV, so I put on a movie. I went to the kitchen to fix me something to eat and saw the letter from my mom on the table.

I wanted to open it to see what she had to say after all these years. Then again, I didn't want to read any more of her lies.
Does she think after all this time she can just write a letter, and everything will be ok?

Where were the letters when I was in foster care? Where was the concern when I took all those pills?

Against my better judgment I opened the letter.

"My dearest Aniya, I just want to start off by saying I love you and I'm so sorry for all the hurt and pain I've caused you. I should not have asked you to do the things I ask you to do. I'm your mother and I should've found a better way to provide for us. I pray you can find it in your heart to forgive me. I really want you back in my life. I am writing to tell you that I went to the doctor last week and they said my tests were abnormal and wanted to do more tests on me. I was hoping you could come with me to my next appointment. My cell phone is off, but I still have the house phone. Please call me after you read this. I love you."

Oh, now she loves me and sorry for what she did.
She can keep being sorry because love doesn't mean anything to me anymore.

PART 2 | FINDING HOPE

Summer

I had just finished making my bed when the guard told me I had a visitor. Don't know who it could be since we only see our lawyer on Tuesdays.

I walked in the room to see a lady standing with her back to me putting papers together. I had never seen her before and wondered why she was here.

"Hi, Summer, my name is Faith and I'm your new lawyer."

"Hello, Ms. Faith, I can't afford a lawyer right now."

"I know sweetie that's why Isaac hired me for you."

"Did you say Isaac hired you on my behalf?"

"Would you like to have a seat and tell me what happened?"

"Yes, ma'am I would love to."

I sat down and told her everything. When I was done, she was looking at me differently.

"You mean to tell me you're here for a man who claims he loves you and he can't find time to come visit you?"

"I just want to finish my time and go home to my family."

"Summer I'm here for you and will get you the justice you deserve."

I just sat there crying thinking how Caleb hasn't come to see me, but Isaac hired a lawyer for me. Faith took my hand and just let me lean on her shoulder.

"I'm sorry for crying, it's just that I'm so grateful to you and Isaac."

"You're more than welcome. Isaac is my god brother and he told me you really needed my help."

"I don't know what I'm going to do with that brother of yours."

"I don't know what to tell you. You know he does what he wants. I am sorry that you're going through this, but we will get you home. Are you taking any classes right now?"

"Yes, I'm enrolled in four now."

"That's wonderful and our next step is to get prepared for your probation hearing."

"What do you need me to do?"

"Just keep God first and believe me when I tell you I have your back."

"I can certainly do that. Thank you again Ms. Faith and tell Isaac I owe him big time."

"Call me Faith and I will definitely tell him."

I walked back to my cell floating on cloud nine. After I got out of the shower, I decided to call Isaac and thank him myself.

"Hi, Mimi, glad to hear your voice."

"Thank you so much for asking your sister to help me."

"No problem, it's my pleasure."

"Can I ask you for a favor?"

"You can ask me anything."

"Can you please not call me Mimi anymore? I hate that name with a passion."

"From now on you will only be Summer to me."

"Thank you so much. I really like your sister, she's so sweet."

"Yes, she is and has been that way since we were young.

Just know that I will always have your back."

"Why are you being so nice to me? Just come out and tell me what you want."

"I don't want anything from you, just trying to give you what you deserve, which is the best."

"Well, our time is up, thanks again for everything Isaac."

"You're very welcome Summer."

My cellmate kept asking me why I was smiling so hard. I told her what Isaac had done for me.

"Girl sounds like Isaac should have been your man instead of Caleb.'

"I know right because he's done more for me than Caleb has ever done."

"If you don't want Isaac, I'll take him off your hands."

Isaac has been on my mind a lot lately. I don't know if he was serious about me not having to pay him back. I'm going to ask again tomorrow just to make sure.

When I finally went to bed, I dreamt about going home and seeing my grandmother.

That was the best sleep I have had since I've been here.

Jurnee

Autumn called me last night to invite me to go to church with her this morning. I just couldn't see myself there with the family that hates me Monday through Saturday but on Sunday loving God.

She called me Thursday night to go to Bible Study with her. I told her I would think about it and get back with her.

I was at the mall looking for something for my birthday when I saw a woman and her daughter looking at prom dresses.

"Mom, can I please get this dress?"

"Jessica, this dress is way over our budget."

"Please mom can we get it? I promise not to ask for anything else."

I felt sorry for her as I saw the disappointed look on her face. I decided to spend my birthday money on something meaningful.

"Hello, my name is Jurnee, and I couldn't help but overhear your conversation about the prom dress."

"Yes ma'am our prom is coming up. My name is Star, and this is my mom, Stacey."

"Nice to meet you both. Star if it's ok with your mom I would love to buy you this dress."

"Ms. Jurnee, I couldn't allow you to do that. This dress cost a lot of money."

"Call me Jurnee and it will be my pleasure. You don't have to pay me back, just get my number and send me some beautiful pictures of Star."

We paid for the dress then ended up going to 3 stores to find shoes to match and some earrings.

We exchanged numbers and I went to the food court to get something to eat. I felt so good on the ride home. It's nice when you can do something for someone else and not expect anything in return.

My aunt called me to see if I could get more things to her party that I'm not even invited to. She caught an attitude when I told her I could help with some things.

Autumn called me back and I decided to go to church with her.

She picked me up around 6:00.

Everyone greeted us with a hug when we walked in church. We found seats up front right when church was about to begin.

The pastor walked up to the pulpit and started praying.

"Shall we pray...Father we thank you for who you are. You're Alpha and Omega the beginning and the end. You're the Bright and Morning Star. Thank You for all You have done for us and all that you will do. We just ask that you have your way in this service. We give you all the honor and the glory. In Jesus' name we pray, Amen."

Pastor Grant talked about forgiveness and how it's not for the people we forgive but for us.

When Bible Study was over Pastor Grant prayed and so many people were saying how they had to forgive others so that they could live the life God has for them.

When we got in the car Autumn took my hand and looked me straight in the face.

"Please do not think you're alone. I know our family doesn't treat you right, always remember that I love you. Don't let them stop you from being the loving person that you are."

"I love you too Autumn and thank you for inviting me to come to church with you. Don't worry they will not steal my joy anymore I just give it all to the Lord."

She dropped me off at home and I told her to text me when she made it home.

I just know this is going to be the best sleep I've had in a long time.

Aniya

Who could be ringing my doorbell at 8:00 at night? I looked through my peephole and saw Amiya.

What in the world is she doing here at my door this time of night?

I opened the door and saw her tears.

Before I knew what was happening, I took her and led her to the living room sofa.

For the longest we didn't say anything. I just let her get out what she was letting go of.

"Aniya I've wanted to come over here for quite some time now, but I was scared you wouldn't allow me to come in or even talk to me."

"Amiya it's just that..."

"Please let me finish. In school you were my only friend, and I did not like what was going on in your home. My mom talked to your worker about adopting you. The paperwork always got messed up. I'm more than sorry for breaking my promise, but I told because I love you and didn't want you in that situation anymore,"

"Thank you for saying that. I've been hurt all these years because I thought you didn't care. It felt like you stabbed me in the back."

"Please believe me I would never do anything on purpose to hurt you."

"I do miss our friendship. I can truly say you were the only person I could count on."

We both started crying and holding each other.

When I really think about it, Amiyah has never told a soul any of my secrets except the one that was causing me harm.

All this time we've been missing out on a beautiful friendship for nothing.

She took my hand and told me to bow my head and close my eyes.

"Father, I thank you for who you are. You are Elohim, El Shaddai, Jehovah Rapha, Jehovah Shalom, and Alpha and Omega. You are everything to us and we love you more than words could ever say. Please touch our hearts and remove anything that's not of you. Fill us back up with love, joy, and peace. Restore our friendship and let it be even better than before. This and all blessings we thank you for in Jesus'

blessed name-Amen."

"Amiya I'm so sorry for hurting you and not speaking to you all these years. It was wrong of me to hold a grudge against you. Thank you for saving my life. If you didn't tell anyone I don't know what would have happened to me."

"No problem, you know I have your back. I will always be here for you."

"I still have your back until the end of time."

We laughed all night and she told me the story of how she was engaged but caught her fiancé cheating.

She also told me how she had a miscarriage stressing over her relationship. Now she was sitting back and waiting for God to send her Boaz.

My heart went out to her, but I know she is strong and I'm going to be here if she needs anything.

We made plans to get together for lunch the next day and she left to get some rest for work.

Father, I thank you for sending my friend back into my life. I'm grateful that you helped me let go of the anger I had.

I closed my eyes and tears started streaming down my face.

These were tears of joy. Joy that I finally had after all these years.

Thank God for healing my heart, spirit, and mind.

Summer

On my way back from one of my classes my cell mate asked if I wanted to go to church in the chapel with her.

I was going to say no but decided to go anyway.

When we walked in there were already twenty or twenty- five people in there.

Everyone stood up and started singing a song I knew, and I joined in.

A lady walked up to the podium and started talking. She looked familiar and I thought I knew her.

"Good evening everyone and if this is your first time joining us my name is Kyra and we're glad you're here. Today I want to talk to you about unforgiveness. Sometimes we harbor pain when someone does wrong by us. When we don't forgive, we make it easy for the enemy to play with our emotions. The Bible tells us that if we want our Heavenly Father to forgive us, we must forgive others who may have wronged us.

Unforgiveness is the worst thing we can have in our hearts. When we forgive and let go of the pain, our hearts are open for God to work on us and through us. How many people here today know you need to ask God for forgiveness or forgive someone?"

About six people raised their hands. I put my head down and raised my hand.

"If you raised your hand, please come up so we can pray together."

We got up and made our way to the front.

"Father, we thank you for another chance to come together in your name. Thank you for being all that you are in our lives. We come in the mighty name of Jesus asking you to search our hearts. If you find anything that's not of You, please remove it. Father, please touch our sisters and heal their hearts and take away their pain. Replace their unforgiveness with forgiveness and keep your arm of protection around them. We love you and it's in Jesus' name we pray-Amen."

We were hugging each other and wiping our eyes.

I'm so glad I came and heard Kyra speak. I thanked her then went to call Caleb.

Can you believe he finally accepted my call?

"What's up Mimi? I was about to get some money together and send it to you."

"Hi, Caleb, I just want to tell you that I forgive you. Don't worry about sending me any money."

"What do you mean you forgive me? Forgive me for what Mimi?"

"I forgive you for not being a man. I forgive myself for being so in love with you. I don't think this is working out between us. My time is about to run out but take care Caleb. Goodbye."

It felt good to tell Caleb I forgave him and meant it. I should have done this a long time ago.

Now it's time to be honest with myself.

I think I do have feelings for Isaac. I have since we were in school.

I called him just to hear his voice.

"Hi Summer, it's nice to hear from you."

"Hi Isaac, I just told Caleb that I forgave him but it's over between us."

"It's about time you let him go. I never knew what you saw in him in the first place."

"Boy you are too much. I just wanted to talk to you before you left. Just want to say thanks again for what you did for me. You didn't have to do it"

"I told you I have your back. Trust me it's not a problem at all."

"Just don't forget about me when you leave."

"How can I forget about you?"

"Stop before you make me blush. My time is up. I hope to see you before you go."

"Trust me you are going to see me real soon."

Jurnee

I was still excited about church service when I woke up this morning.

I never knew she noticed how our family treated me.

"Thank You, Father, for forgiving me and helping me to forgive and let go."

After I got the rest of the things my Aunt Elizabeth asked for her party, I went to get the cake.

She changed the cake order and got the biggest and most expensive one.

I pulled up to my aunt's house and stayed in the car for a few minutes to clear my head.

When I walked inside everyone stopped talking. That's how I know I'm the subject of discussion.

"Hello everyone. Aunt Elizabeth here is everything I said I would get for you. I have a couple more things in the car."

I walked outside and Autumn came to help me.

"Have a great time everyone I have to get going."

I was waiting for a "Thank you" or "You don't have to go', but I didn't get either one.

"Jurnee you can't stay for a little while?" Autumn asked me.

"No sweetie I wish I could, but I really have to go."

My family looked at me with so much hate in their eyes.

"Aunt Elizabeth, you're not going to tell Jurnee anything?"

"Autumn, if she wants to leave, she can go."

I turned to walk outside but Autumn grabbed my hand.

"She did just buy almost everything for your party."

"Autumn it's ok I really need to get going."

"No Jurnee please stay. Aunt Betty, is there anything you want to tell Jurnee?"

"No, there is nothing I need to tell her,"my mom replied.

"What exactly do you think we have to tell her?" Aunt Elizabeth asked.

Autumn's face turned so red I thought she was going to explode.

"First, you can tell her thank you for all your party stuff she brought. Second, I heard you guys talking last night on the porch. She has the right to know the truth."

My mom and aunt looked at each other more than at me. I did

not know what was going on, but I really wanted to leave.

"Since you guys not going to say anything. Jurnee, do you remember Ms. Jackie from our old neighborhood?"

"Yes, she was very sweet and nice to us."

"I heard them on the porch talking about how Ms. Jackie is your real mom. She had you at an early age and asked Aunt Betty to take care of you until she got on her feet."

I looked at my mom and Aunt Elizabeth with tears and my eyes. They couldn't look me in my face.

"She was paying Aunt Betty every month when she got paid. She even helped pay for you to go to college."

"Mom, is this true?"

"Jurnee, I just didn't know how or when to tell you."

"Maybe before she died would have been the perfect time."

I felt myself breathing harder and faster and I wanted to scream.

"I always felt I didn't belong in this family. Never knew why you guys hated me so much. Now that I know the truth, everything makes perfect sense now."

I hugged Autumn and turned to the rest of the family.

"I forgive you all and release the hurt and pain that you have caused me. I pray you ask God for forgiveness one day. Autumn I love you and thank you for telling me."

I walked outside and Autumn followed behind me.

"What are you going to do now Jurnee?"

"I'm going to talk to Ms. Jackie's niece and see if she can give me more information. I'll text you later and thanks again."

Today I choose victory and not hatred. Now I know why I felt like I didn't belong, because I really don't belong to that family.

I cannot wait to start this new chapter of my life.

Aniya

Amiya and I have talked every day since the night she came over to my house. We even made plans to take a girl's trip.

I read my mom's letter again. Still can't believe she wrote me after all this time.

Even though she wants something, it still feels good to have gotten the letter.

When Amiya called, I decided to tell her about the letter.

"Guess who sent me a letter?"

"Please tell me who it's from."

"My mom wrote and told me she has to get a test done and she's sorry for what happened when I was younger. She wants me to go with her to her doctor appointment."

"Wow! That's deep Aniya. Are you going to go with her?"

"I forgive her and yes I'm going to go with her."

"You know I'm here for the both of you if you need anything."

"Her appointment is tomorrow at ten o' clock if you can come with us."

"You know I got you just tell me what time to be ready."

"I'll pick you up at nine thirty and then we can head over there."

"Ok I'll be ready. I'll see you in the morning."

"Goodnight and thanks again."

"Goodnight."

I took a shower and then found something to eat.

I couldn't sleep so I decided to read a book. I picked up the Bible my grandmother had given me.

"God, I don't know how things will turn out tomorrow, but I ask you to help get our relationship where it needs to be. Thank you for sending Amiya back into my life. Please heal my mother. In Jesus name-Amen."

I went to sleep and felt so at peace. Since I let the past go, I feel so much better.

I woke up the next morning and got dressed then text Amiya that I was on my way.

Today is going to be a great day because I'm expecting great things.

"Good morning Aniya, how are you feeling?"

"I'm good. I can't wait to see my mom. It's been a long time since I've spoken to her."

We arrived at the doctor's office and my mom was already in the back waiting for her doctor.

Amiya told me to go to the back with my mom and she would wait in the waiting room.

The nurse brought me to the back, and I just took a deep breath.

When I walked in the room my mom started smiling.

"Aniya, thank you so much for coming."

"Hi mom, thanks for asking me to be here with you."

I walked over to my mom and gave her a hug and kiss. When I sat down her doctor walked in.

"Good morning Dr. Elijah, how are you?"

"Good morning Ms. Heather. I'm good. Who do you have here with you today?"

"This is my daughter Aniya. Aniya, this is Dr. Elijah."

"Hi Aniya, it's nice to meet you."

"It's nice to meet you as well, Dr. Elijah."

I caught my mom looking in my direction and she started smiling.

I really hope she doesn't try to play cupid.

"Well Ms. Heather, we have some great news. I sent your lab work to the lab, and they saw a small tumor and we will be able to remove it. Our next step is to schedule your day for surgery."

"Thank You, Jesus! Oh my God thank You! This is an amazing news doc."

"Yes, it is. I'm going to look at the surgery schedule and the nurse will give you all the information. I'll see you soon."

"Thank you again."

My mom and I started screaming and clapping. The nurse had to come make sure everything was ok.

"Baby if you're not busy the day of surgery, can you please come with me?"

"Of course, I will mom."

"I love you and thanks again for being here."

"I love you too mom."

I went to the waiting room and told Amiya the good news.

Of course, she wanted to be there with us.

What an awesome God we serve!!

Summer

After I got off the phone with Isaac, the guard told me I had a visitor.

When I went to see who it was Isaac was standing there with a big smile on his face.

"I told you I'll see you soon."

"You play too doggone much. What am I going to do with you?"

"Guess all you can do is love me."

"What if I really do love you?"

"That makes it even better. I wanted to come see you before I leave in the morning."

"Thanks, that means so much to me. I'm so happy for you."

"Thank you. Faith said that your hearing is coming up and she really thinks the board will grant your probation."

"That will be a blessing."

"Yes, it will be a huge blessing."

"Isaac, I don't know how to thank you enough."

"Just keep being the sweet Summer that I know."

"I hope you come visit when you move."

"You know that I am. I can't have anyone making moves on you."

"No, we really can't have that."

"I have to get going so I can finish packing. You know you can call me anytime."

"Thank you from the bottom of my heart."

"I love you Summer."

"I love you too Isaac."

When the guard looked away, Isaac gave me a quick kiss.

I was the happiest I had been in a while. I walked back to my cell singing and skipping.

My probation hearing was a couple of days later. I went to my hearing confident that I already had the victory.

I thought I was going to receive three years' probation instead I received six months.

The board said my good behavior, going to class, and working hard worked in my favor.

Look at God!!!!!!!

"Ms. Faith, thank you for helping me. I'm so grateful for all you've done for me."

"Please call me Faith. I just did my job to get a good woman out of a situation where she didn't belong."

"I thank God for you. I don't know what I would have done without you and Isaac."

"When God is for you, who can be against you?"

"Amen to that. I can't wait to call Isaac and give him the good news."

"Tell him I said hello. I'm going to get going but call me if you need anything."

"I surely will and thanks again Faith."

"You're more than welcome Summer."

I ran to the phone to call Isaac.

"Hi again my love. How did your hearing go?"

"Your god sister is an amazing lawyer. I got six months' probation and I'm coming home tomorrow. Just waiting for the judge to sign the papers."

"Thank God for that."

"What time do you leave tomorrow?"

'I leave early in the morning. I promise to come straight to you when I get back."

"That works for me. Is it ok if I leave the money you gave me to my cellmate? No one comes to see her, and I know how that feels."

"That's why I love you. Always thinking of others and not yourself. Of course, you can."

"Thanks. Love you."

"I love you too, Summer."

I told my cellmate about the money I would be leaving her. She was so excited and told me to thank Isaac for her.

I'm going to sleep so good tonight knowing I'm going home in the morning.

If I can even manage to get some sleep. I'm so excited right now!

"Father, thank You for all your many blessings!"

Jurnee

I found Ms. Jackie's niece Lisa number and asked her if I could come by to talk to her.

She said yes and I texted Autumn to let her know I was going over there.

"Hi Jurnee, come on in. Please excuse the mess. I'm getting things together for our annual clothes give away. You can have a seat."

"Thanks for allowing me to come over. I just heard something, and I hope you can help me clear some things up."

"So, they finally told you about my aunt?"

"Lisa, you knew this whole time and didn't tell me?"

"My aunt told me before she passed and made me promise not to say anything. She said that was your mom's job."

"I just want to know why she never told me anything."

"My aunt did love you Jurnee. That's mainly the reason you're my only friend that got away with everything."

Even I had to laugh at that statement. That was very true.

"Why didn't she come get me when she got her stuff together?"

"She didn't want to take you from the only family you knew."

"I wish she would have. Do you have any pictures of her that I can have?"

"Yes, I do. Follow me to her room."

Her room was like two hotel suites put together. She had great taste and her closet was amazing also.

"This is your mother's house you can have whatever you want of hers. I'll be in the living room if you need me."

"Thank you so much Lisa."

"You're welcome cousin."

When Lisa called me cousin it felt real, and I knew she meant it.

It was an awesome feeling to have someone to want me around.

I found some pictures of her and my mom Betty. I sat on her bed and looked at all her photo albums.

Lisa knocked on the door and peeped in the room.

"Aunt Jackie's lawyer read her will yesterday and she left you this house and four safety deposit boxes."

"Lisa, are you playing with me right now?"

"No, I am not. I was packing my things and leaving you all the keys."

"You know you don't have to leave right?"

"Thank you but with the money she left me I bought a house."

"I'm so happy for you."

We hugged each other and I started crying. Lisa asked me what was wrong, and I told her how I have been feeling like I am not a part of my family since I was little.

"Cousin, I'm sorry you had to go through that. Now you're with your family and we love you."

"I love you too Lisa."

I couldn't wait to call Autumn and tell her everything.

I'm so glad I allowed God to help me forgive and let go of the past hurt and pain.

Now I can enjoy my happiness.

When Autumn came, I showed her around the house.

We helped Lisa put the rest of her things into the U-haul.

We went out to the back yard to look around, and it was bigger than any yard I've seen.

I think I'm going to enjoy my real family.

Aniya

Amiya and I are in the waiting room waiting for the nurse to give us an update on my mom.

I'm a little scared, but I know God has his hands around her.

"Thanks again for coming with us Amiya. It really means a lot to the both of us."

"No need to thank me. That's what friends are for."

We were laughing and clowning when the nurse came.

"Just wanted to let you know the surgery went great. Your mother is in recovery, and I'll take you to see her in about thirty minutes."

"Thank you."

"You're welcome. See you in a little while."

I closed my eyes and thanked God for bringing my mom out of surgery.

When Amiya went to the restroom, I heard a commotion. I turned my head to see one of the men my mom pimped me out to.

He walked over to me with flowers in his hands.

"Hi, the nurse told me that you're Heather's daughter. I'm her friend Jacob. Did they give you an update on her yet?"

I thought I would scream and yell at him and ask him why he did those things to me.

I felt this calm spirit over me, and I just looked at him and smiled.

"Hi Mr. Jacob. The nurse said the surgery went well and I can go see her in about thirty minutes."

"Thank God. I'm on my way to work and I'm running late. Can you give her these flowers for me and let her know I'm praying for her recovery?"

"I will and thank you for stopping by."

He left and I took out my book to read. I heard voices but couldn't see what it was.

Amiya came back laughing.

"What is so funny?"

"Girl a man's wife, fiancé, and three girlfriends all came to the hospital to see him."

"We're going to pray for him and that cheating spirit of his."

"He's going to need more than prayer if his wife breaks away from the security guard."

We laughed so hard until tears rolled down our cheeks.

The nurse came and got us to bring us to my mom's room.

We walked in and could tell she was in a lot of pain.

She could barely move and was trying to talk.

"Mom please don't try to move. Get some rest, we will be here when you wake up."

I kissed her on the forehead, and she smiled then drifted off to sleep.

The next thing I heard was chairs flying and people cussing each other out.

I looked out the door and saw a group of women fighting.

Amiya had to leave but told me she was coming back later.

I put the flowers that Mr. Jacob left for my mom by her bed.

I took my book out and started to read. I would look up at my mom every now and then.

I fell asleep in the chair and woke up with a crick in my neck.

The nurse came in to check mom's vital signs.

I asked if the cafeteria was open, but it was closed.

I texted Amiya to bring me something to eat when was on her way back.

My mom would wake up and fall back to sleep.

She woke up again and tried talking.

"Thank you, baby, for being here with me."

"It's not a problem mom. Now go back to sleep."

She smiled and drifted back to sleep.

Amiya came with some food, and we ate and laughed and talked.

I was so happy my best friend was here with us.

Thank You, Heavenly Father, for another blessing.

PART 3 | THE ART OF FORGIVENESS

Summer

I got up early and started getting my things together. I prayed then took my shower and thought about who I could call to pick me up.

I thought about calling Caleb but decided to walk home.

Around ten o'clock the guard came and brought me to the office.

I signed my release papers and waved goodbye to my girls.

The guard walked me outside and I saw Faith waiting for me.

"Hi Faith. Did your god brother ask you to pick me up?"

"Hi Summer. You know he did. Do you want to grab a bite to eat before I bring you home?"

"I would love to but I'm a little short on cash."

"Don't worry it's on me."

We got to the restaurant and pulled into an empty parking spot.

When we walked inside the waitress brought us back to the private room.

She opened the door and people shouted, 'Welcome Home Summer'.

Someone came up behind me and covered my eyes.

"Guess who?"

"I don't know. Wait, I know that voice. Is that you Kelsey?"

She removed her hands and I turned around and saw her.

I screamed so loud I think I hurt her ears.

"What are you doing here Kelsey?"

"I wouldn't have missed this for anything in the world."

"How did you know I was coming home today?"

"I emailed her and told her what was going on," Isaac replied.

I looked up and saw Isaac standing in the door with flowers.

"I thought you left to go to your uncle's?"

"My interview was last week. Yes, I got the job if you wanted to know."

"Congratulations!"

Next thing I know Isaac had gotten down on one knee.

"Summer I love you and want to spend the rest of my life with you. I have loved you since we were in school, and you have always been the one that got away. Will you marry me?"

"Yes Isaac. I'll marry you!"

He placed the ring on my finger, and I started to cry.

He hugged me and walked me over to where my grandmother was.

"I'm so happy to see you granny. I love you so much."

"I love you too baby. Thank God you're finally home where you belong."

Kelsey took her fork and clanked her glass.

"I want to make a toast to the most beautiful person I know. Summer you have a big heart and I thank God that you're in my life. I love you, my Sue. To Summer."

Everyone raised their glass and said, 'To Summer.'

We ordered our food, and everyone wanted to see my ring.

I walked over to Isaac because I had some concerns.

"Isaac, we need to talk. How can we get married if you're moving out of state?"

"Baby you don't worry about your pretty little head. I got the position in the next town from where we live."

"I'm so happy right now."

"I'm happy as well baby."

Our food came and it far exceeded my expectations.

I was grateful my grandmother was letting me stay with her until my probation was over.

This is one of the greatest days of my life!!

Jurnee

My mom Becky heard that my mom had left me her house and some money. I wonder where she heard that.

The family attitude toward me changed in a blink of an eye.

Every day they call and check on me. Wonder why the sudden change of heart?

Deep down I always knew I belonged to another family.

I mean how can you have so much hate for one person?

Looking at the pictures of my mom, I do favor her a lot.

I can remember coming over for sleepovers with Lisa on the weekends.

One night Lisa invited us over and we snuck out the house. My mom Jackie found out and called everyone parents except for mine. It sounds good to say to my mom!!

She came on the porch where I was and told me something I have not forgotten until this day.

"Jurnee, I want you to know that I'm disappointed in you and Lisa."

"Yes, ma'am I know and I'm really sorry."

"I know you are, that's why I'm letting you stay."

I always felt safe and wanted whenever I came around.

There was a picture in her room of Autumn, Lisa, and I.

I picked up the Bible that was sitting on her nightstand.

An envelope with my name on it dropped out of it.

I looked at the date and she had written it five years ago.

"Dear Jurnee,

I'm sorry it took me so long to tell you this. Betty is not your mother, I am. When I had you, I was young and not working so I asked her to take care of you until I got on my feet. I thought that was the best thing for you. When I did get on my feet, I didn't want to take you from the only life you ever knew. I am so proud of you and all that you've accomplished. You graduated high school and went to college. I never wanted you to hate me or think that I didn't want you. I pray one day you can forgive me. I love you so much Jurnee. Keep being the woman God has created you to be."

Love always,
Jackie (your mother)

I must have read the letter about ten times.

I do love you mom and I could never hate you. I wish you were still here with us.

When Autumn came over, I let her read the letter.

"Ms. Jackie really loved you."

"I just wish I knew sooner that she was my mom. I could have told her how much I love her."

"Jurnee, she already knew I promised you."

I showed her the pictures I found with all of us in them.

"I wish I was still that size."

"You want to be a size six your whole life in Autumn?"

"Yes ma'am I do."

We started laughing so hard my head began to hurt.

Lisa came in and we showed her the pictures.

My mom was truly one of a kind.

I'm keeping this letter in my purse so it will be with me all the time.

Aniya

The doctor discharged my mom and I brought her home. I decided to stay with her for a while to make sure she would be fine.

Amiya stopped by every day to see if we needed anything.

A couple of my mom friends came by throughout the day.

I fell asleep on the sofa and checked on my mom when I woke up.

When I was getting her medicine ready my phone started to ring.

It was Amiya's mom, Ms. Brenda.

"Hi Ms. Brenda, how are you?"

"I'm good Aniya, how is Heather feeling?"

"She's ok. Her medicine is helping with the pain."

"Thank God, they gave her something that works. I made her some soup. I will send it to Amiya. Please don't forget I'm here if you guys need anything."

"Thank you, Ms. Brenda."

"You're welcome. Tell her I called to check on her."

"Yes, ma'am I will."

I heard my mom moaning so I brought her medicine.

When I walked in, she was crying and holding her chest.

I called 911 and EMS came and checked her out.

They said her blood pressure was extremely high and took her to the E.R.

When we got there the doctor ran a test on her.

They decided to change the dose of her medicine. Once they did that her blood pressure went back to normal.

She stayed overnight so they could monitor her.

I text Amiya to tell her what was going on.

Once I got comfortable in the chair, I asked the nurse for a pillow and a blanket.

Seems like every time I fell asleep one of the nurses would come turn on the light to check on mom.

I was surprised when I woke up, I did not have a crick in my neck.

The doctor said mom was doing much better and would be able to go home today.

Thank You, Jesus!!

Amiya came and picked us up and brought us home.

She brought the soup her mom made so I warmed some up for

mom.

Amiya helped me put mom in bed and we went to watch movies and popped some popcorn.

The doorbell rang and Amiya went to answer it for me.

"Aniya, there's someone at the door for you. He says his name is Kyle."

What is my ex-boyfriend doing here? I haven't spoken to him in two years.

"Aniya how are you?"

"Hi Kyle, I'm good."

"I heard about Ms. Heather and wanted to stop by and see her."

"Thank you. She is doing better and just came from the hospital this morning. She's resting but I will tell her you came by."

"I also wanted to tell you that I miss you and I still think about you."

"You miss me, but you couldn't call or text?"

"You made it clear not to contact you."

"Yes, I did say that huh?"

We both smiled and he started laughing.

"Do you think we can go to lunch or dinner tomorrow?"

"I can ask Amiya to stay with mom for a little while."

"That sounds great."

"Do you have the same number?"

"Yes I do."

"I'll let you know if I can make it after I talk with my friend."

"Ok tell Ms. Heather she's in my prayers."

I closed the door and Amiya was standing looking at me with a cheetah smile on her face.

"Text him and tell him you can go Friday. So, who exactly is this Kyle fellow?"

"He's my ex and we have been broken up for two years."

"That was sweet of him to come check on your mom."

"Yes, it was."

I walked past her to the living room so she could not see me smiling. I felt my cheeks turn red.

That man still gives me butterflies after all this time.

Summer

When I got to my grandmother's house, I took the longest bubble bath.

It felt so good to be there alone and not with twenty other people.

I fell asleep and when I got out of the tub my toes and fingers were wrinkled.

My grandmother was on her porch swing, so I went and sat down with her.

"Granny thanks again for letting me stay with you."

"Baby it's not a problem at all. I just thank God you're safe and sound."

We talked and laughed for what seemed like forever.

Faith picked me up for my appointment with my probation officer.

Isaac asked her if she could bring me since he had to work.

On our way home she brought me to the store to get some things for my grandmother.

Isaac called me while I was cooking.

"Hello my beautiful Queen."

"Hello my handsome King."

"I cannot wait to get off so I can come see you. How did it go with your probation officer?"

"It went really well. I'm cooking so my grandmother can eat."

"Are you going to save a brother a plate?"

"You know that I got you."

"I love you."

"I love you too Isaac."

I finished the food then fixed our plates.

After we ate my grandmother showed me some pictures of when I was younger.

"Granny, I look just like you when I was a baby."

"Yes, you did get your beautiful looks from me."

We laughed so hard my stomach started to hurt.

I put the food away and cleaned the kitchen.

Faith called me and asked if I wanted to go to a party with her tomorrow night.

I told her I would love to go but I didn't have anything to wear.

I went to the living room and watched a movie on TV.

I'm not going to miss getting up at five am every morning.

Freedom is such a wonderful thing.

Faith came and picked me up and brought me something to wear to the party.

She told me to get whatever I wanted.

I only got two pairs of jeans, two shirts, and a pair of shoes.

Faith got the dates mixed up for the party it was tonight, so she dropped me off to get ready.

We had such a good time at her cousin's house. It was nice to be around women without any drama going on.

I'm so glad Faith invited me to come with her.

When I got home, I checked on my grandmother and texted Isaac.

I'm so thankful to be home!!

Jurnee

I opened the deposit boxes my mother had left for me.

There was money, jewelry, savings bonds, and her passport.

Tomorrow I am going to pay off Autumn's truck and that will be her birthday present.

I just need to find out what Lisa needs.

I said my prayers then went to sleep.

I woke up, said my prayers then went to the dealership.

I asked for Mr. David because I knew that's who sold Autumn her truck.

"Good morning Mr. David. I'm Jurnee, Autumn Green's cousin."

"Good morning Jurnee. What can I do for you today?"

"I wanted to see if I can pay off Autumn's truck and you mail her the title?"

"That's real thoughtful of you. Follow me to my office."

Mr. David pulled up the information and Autumn only owed twelve thousand dollars.

After I made the payment, he gave me a receipt and made a separate one for Autumn.

I was glad when he promised not to let it be known that I was the one who paid the balance.

On my way home I stopped at the store and saw Lisa's best friend. I asked her if she knew what Lisa would want.

She said Lisa has been trying to go on a vacation for a while.

I think I will surprise her and Autumn with a cruise.

I moved into my mother's house, and it felt so good.

I wish I could have spent more time with her before she passed away.

After I got out of the shower I got on my laptop and looked up dates for a cruise and a nice place we could go.

Someone kept ringing my doorbell like it was going out of style this morning.

I looked through the peephole and saw Autumn.

"I received a phone call from Mr. David at the car dealership to come to his office. I get there and he gives me a receipt and the title to my truck."

"That's great. One less bill you have to pay."

"Jurnee, did you have anything to do with this?"

I walked away so I wouldn't have to think of a lie.

"Jurnee answered me right now. Did you do this?"

"Yes, I did Autumn. I wanted to show you how thankful I am that you had my back all these years."

She grabbed me and hugged me so tight.

"Thank you, I just don't know when I will be able to pay it all back to you."

"You don't owe me anything, that's your birthday present."

"Thank You, Father!"

When Autumn left, I went to lie down because I was a little tired. My phone started ringing and when I looked at it my Aunt Elizabeth name popped up.

She found out about my money and asked me for ten thousand dollars.

She wanted to pay off her living room and bedroom sets.

When I went to the store, I found out she only owed five thousand dollars.

I paid it for her because there is no hatred in my heart.

I booked the cruise the days I knew the three of us could go.

I text the girls to tell them what I had done.

They decided to stay the night at my house the night before so we could get ready together and leave.

This is going to be an awesome trip.

Aniya

Kyle came early to pick me up. I told my mom I was going for a while and Amiya was going to be here with her.

She told me to have fun and not to worry about her.

I walked outside and Kyle opened the car door for me.

We pulled into the restaurants' parking lot, and I see this is the same restaurant I would ask him to go to, but he never had time.

He got out of the car and opened my door for me.

When we walked in the waiter brought us to our table and gave us a menu. He took our drink order and gave us a minute to see what we wanted to eat.

"Aniya do you see anything you like?"

"Not yet but thanks for bringing me here. I know it's a little pricey."

"Nothing is too good for you. I should have brought you here a long time ago."

The waiter came back with our drinks and took our order.

I looked up and Kyle was just staring at me.

"What? Do I have something on my face?"

"No, I'm just seeing how beautiful you still are."

"Stop playing with me Kyle."

"I'm serious Aniya. I want to apologize for how things turned out between us. I really want us to work things out."

I looked at him for a minute and put my head down.

When we first got together things were great until his ex-started to come around.

I never caught them doing anything. She just didn't know her place and he wasn't man enough to tell her what it was.

I told him since he still wanted her around there was no need for me to be in his life.

"Kyle, I loved you, I just didn't want to play second string to your ex."

"I'm sorry I should have fought for us instead of letting you walk away. I miss you and I still love you."

"I just don't want another ex to come between us again."

"Aniya, I love you and I'm going to do whatever it takes to win your trust back."

I wanted to believe him so bad I just don't want to get hurt again. I did love him, and I knew he would not do anything to hurt me.

"Kyle, if we do this again, we will always be honest with each other."

"I promise to be honest and to never let anyone or anything come between us."

Our food came and we ate and enjoyed ourselves.

When the check came Kyle paid it and left our waiter a nice tip.

When he brought me home, he came inside to talk with my mom.

She was happy to see him because she always wanted us to get married.

I walked Kyle outside and thanked him again for a good time.

He kissed my hand and told me he would call me when he made it home.

After Amiya left, I went into my mom's room, and we talked all night.

My mom drifted off to sleep and I stayed in her room.

I started thinking about Kyle and the good time we had.

I'm glad Amiya and I are friends again. I was mad at myself for letting so much time pass us by.

She saved my life, but I didn't see it that way when I was younger.

Summer

I can't believe I'm planning a wedding!!

The years I spent with Caleb I could have been with a man that absolutely loves me.

So glad God showed me his true colors.

I put the clothes in the dryer, and I hear a car outside. I look and I see Caleb getting out of his car.

I dialed Isaac's number but didn't say anything so he could hear what was going on.

"What's up Mimi? Why did I have to hear from the streets that you were home?"

"Caleb my name is Summer, and we are not together anymore. That means I'm no longer a concern of yours."

Next thing I know two of Isaac's friends pulled up in the driveway.

"Oh, it's like that? Your man sending people to protect you?"

"I don't have to explain myself to you."

"Girl, you're going to make me come over there and beat the brakes off you."

One of Isaac's friends got out of the car.

"I don't think you want this. I suggest you get in your car, leave, and never come back here."

"Mimi it's like that?"

"Please leave Caleb, I don't want you here."

"The lady has spoken, and your time is up."

Caleb got in his car and sped off.

Isaac's friends looked to see if I was straight and said they would stay for a while to make sure Caleb didn't come back.

I picked up the phone to talk to Isaac.

"Baby, are you ok?"

"Yes I am. Thanks for staying on the phone and sending someone to check on me."

"You know I have your back."

"I love you, Isaac."

"I love you too, my Queen."

When I got off the phone with Isaac, I called Faith to tell her what happened.

Thank God my grandmother was sleeping.

I went inside and started thinking about wedding plans again. I asked Kelsey to be my matron of honor and Faith to be my maid of honor.

I want a big wedding because I'm only getting married one time.

We set a date and reserved the church and venue.

My grandmother, Kelsey, and Faith helped a lot with the planning.

I'm glad I ask God to heal my heart and help me to forgive.

Unforgiveness could have robbed me of the blessing God had for me.

Jurnee

We woke up at 4:30 to get dressed and get our stuff together.

We had to be at the airport for 7:00.

Our cab came on time, and we headed out.

The airport wasn't as crowded as I thought it would be.

After making sure everything was good, we were finally called to get on the plane.

We got off the plane and found our cabin on the cruise ship.

When the ship took off, I thought I was going to be sick.

We arrived at our destination and got off the ship.

After shopping and doing some sightseeing, it was time to get on the ship and go to our next stop.

When we were getting back on the ship Aunt Elizabeth texted Autumn and told her she better bring her something back. The nerve of her to be so demanding. She could have asked her and not demand something.

This cruise is what we all needed to wind down and have some fun.

When we made it back to the airport the same cab picked us up.

We went to sleep after we got to my house.

I woke up and saw Autumn crying in the living room.

"Autumn what's wrong sweetie?"

She showed me the text she got from my mom and Aunt Elizabeth.

"Autumn I know Jurnee gave you some of that money. I need my house note paid and Becky needs a new car. Remember who helped raise you."

God help me to hold my tongue and remove this anger from me. "Autumn, don't feel like you have to do anything for them because they cannot manage their money and pay bills on time."

"I'm so tired of them acting like I owe them my life."

"Well, you're moving in here with me and there is nothing they can say about it."

"Jurnee I couldn't impose on you like that."

"You were the only one who treated me like family. You have always been there for me and now it's time I returned the favor."

When we went to get Autumn things my aunt tried to give her a hard time, but I stepped in.

"Autumn is leaving with me, and she will not be returning here. That was wrong for you to demand that she help you guys. Not being disrespectful, just telling you how we feel."

We went to Autumn's room and got all her things.

They talked about us like dogs but when God is for you who can be against you!!!

"You're my cousin and family sticks together."

"I love you too Jurnee."

It felt so good to have Autumn here with me at my mother's house-well my house. Lisa stopped by on her way home from work every day.

I thank God every day for healing my heart and helping me to forgive.

Glad God took away my bitterness so I can live in peace with my real family-Autumn and Lisa.

Aniya

Thank God mom is up and moving around the house.

She is looking so much better, and her nurse comes twice a week to check on her.

Kyle has been coming over and helping me take care of her.

“Thanks again for helping me with mom. It means the world to the both of us.”

“No problem at all my love.”

I walked him to his truck then went to check on mom.

When I walked in her room, she had a big smile on her face.

“Aniya, when are you planning this wedding?”

“What wedding are you talking about mom?”

“The love you two have for each other can start a fire.”

We both had to laugh at that even though it was true.

I told her how we decided to give it another try.

“I’m so happy and thank him for me for stopping by to check on me.”

“I will mom, now get some rest.”

I called Amiya and told her that Kyle and I were back together.

“All I know is that I'm your Maid of Honor.”

“How are you going to assume that we are getting married?”

“You light up every time he calls, or you talk about him.”

“It’s amazing that he still has that effect on me after all this time.”

I got off the phone and went to take a bath.

I was watching videos on my phone when Kyle sent me a text.

“Just want to tell you how happy I am that you are back in my life. You are my favorite gift from God. If it’s ok, I would like to come see your mom tomorrow. I love you.’

I told him he could stop by, and he said he should be over by 2:00.

I got out of the tub and checked on my mom. She was sleeping so I went to the living room.

I watched a movie and fell asleep. I don’t know what time it was, but I woke up to the smell of food being cooked.

Amiya had used her key I had given her and was in the kitchen cooking breakfast.

Kyle texted me if he could come over this morning.

When he came in, he wanted to bring my mom her food.

"Good morning Ms. Heather, here is your breakfast."

"Thank you for bringing it to me."

"I really stopped by because I wanted to talk to you about something important. I love Aniya and I will never hurt her. I wanted to ask you if I can have your daughter's hand in marriage."

"Thank you for being a good man and asking me. Yes, you can."

"Aniya, can you come into your mother's room for a minute please?"

"Is everything ok with my mom?"

I walked in the room and Kyle was on one knee.

"I love you Aniya more than anything and I want to spend the rest of my life with you. Will you marry me?"

"Of course, I will marry you!"

It feels so good to have God's mercy and grace.

To top it off He gave me another chance with the three most important people in my life.

ABOUT THE AUTHOR

Tanisha Hall lives in Gonzales, Louisiana, with her son Skyler Hall. She's a 1999 graduate of Plaquemine Senior High, and she attended Southern University A&M College. She loves writing, reading, having a movie night with her son, and spending time with her family and friends. Her love for writing started when she was young and has been writing since 2006. Tanisha has seen her share of heartache being used, lied on, talked about, put in foster care, and left to take the blame. While reading this book, she prays that you find your Art of Forgiveness and live the best life God has for you.

Made in the USA
Las Vegas, NV
06 October 2021

31809645R00039